In the Snow

by Sharon Phillips Denslow

pictures by Nancy Tafuri

Greenwillow Books

An Imprint of HarperCollinsPublishers

Watercolor paints were used to prepare the full-color art.
The text type is Venetian.

Library of Congress Cataloging-in-Publication Data
Denslow, Sharon Phillips.
In the snow / written by Sharon Phillips Denslow ;
illustrated by Nancy Tafuri.
  p. cm.
"Greenwillow Books."
Summary: Forest animals come out after a fresh snow to
eat the seeds a thoughtful child has scattered on the ground.

ISBN 0-06-059683-X (trade). ISBN 0-06-059684-8 (lib. bdg.)
1. Forest animals—Juvenile fiction. [1. Forest animals—Fiction.
2. Animal feeding—Fiction. 3. Snow—Fiction.] I. Tafuri, Nancy,
ill. II. Title.
PZ10.3.D397In 2005 [E]—dc22 2003056861

First Edition 10 9 8 7 6 5 4 3 2 1

Greenwillow Books

To all the children in the snow
scattering seeds high and low
~S.P.D.

To Tom, a bird-lover
~N.T.

Someone's coming
in the snow
for the seeds
left high

and low~
millet, thistle,
corn dropped so.

Here comes
chickadee,

sparrow,

cardinal,

crow.

Someone's coming
in the snow~

red squirrel
and gray,
climbing high
and running
low.

Someone's coming
in the snow~
bunnies hopping
soft and slow.

Field mouse stops
as shadows grow.

Last to show
in the night,
in the snow~

Old Man Possum,
eyes aglow,
dark shape
crunching
seeds in snow.

In the morning,
in the snow,
look who came
and didn't go.

Old Man Possum
in the tree

waits for more seeds
brought by me.